Indian Softball Summer

Indian Softball Summer

or

"KICKAPOOS NEVER SAY GOOD-BYE"

RONALD G. BLISS

ILLUSTRATED BY WILLIAM MOYERS

DODD, MEAD & COMPANY
NEW YORK

To my wife, Janie,
and my two sons, Eric and Kirk

Chapter 1

A giant tumbleweed hugging the city-limit sign of Ludell, Kansas, was Rand's real welcome to the heartland. He gazed past the sign to a small circular ball park and the three brightly colored bases on the infield.

"We wanted to lighten up the infield a bit," said Clyde, "so we painted first base yellow, second red, and third blue." Rand's cousin looked proud. "How's that for a welcome to northwest Kansas?"

Rand didn't answer. He stared instead at the first softball diamond he had ever seen. It was sure different from the glimpse of Shea Stadium he had caught when his jet took off earlier that same day.

"Wanted to show you some of that New York Met spirit hangs over the prairie." Clyde wheeled the pickup into the entrance to the ball park and turned off the ignition.

Rand looked around the field in this land his father called "the kingdom of soapweeds and coyotes." Deep gulleys and slashing canyons hid behind a freshly painted red snow fence in the outfield. It promised to be an interesting summer.

Clyde broke the silence. "Indians used to camp right on the ball park. We've found arrowheads and even a tomahawk behind the snow fence. I guess they came because of the spring over there." He pointed toward the base of a high bluff.

The sand-colored bluff was dotted with giant soapweeds and small clumps of buffalo grass. Its sides glowed in the rays of the setting sun. The cousins were quiet as they waited for the other members of the team to arrive.

"Why do you play softball?" asked Rand after awhile. "Baseball's a better game. It's for healthy people. Requires more skill. Softball's a game for old-timers and girls."

"We all like baseball, Rand, but people here think softball is a better game. There's more hitting and action, and it's easier for most people to play than baseball."

Rand turned to study his cousin. Clyde was large with big hands—much like the giant hoofs of a plowhorse—and shoulders more like a full-back than a softball player. His red hair and the freckles across his nose and cheeks made him look like Tom Sawyer. He was the stereotyped picture of the All-American boy, the farm boy. Clyde even had a chipped front tooth, so that each time he smiled he looked as if he were stepping out of a Norman Rockwell picture.

"I was wondering," said Rand, breaking the silence. "How come there isn't an adult managing instead of you? What I mean is, most teams have an older guy working with kids. I know you are good and know the game, but usually parents want someone older to manage."

"We had an older man managing," said Clyde, "but Mr. Focke had a heart attack last year. He hasn't been too well ever since. I managed the last couple of games and I guess most people were happy."

"What do you think the players and other people will think about an outsider coming in to be co-manager and telling them what to do?" asked Rand.

"No sweat," said Clyde. "As long as they know you want to help the team, you'll be in no trouble."

He ran his hand through his red hair. "Guess I had better tell you how we play slow-pitch softball. The pitcher can't throw the ball hard, and he has to loft it some. Very few guys strike out, so that really puts the pressure on the defense." Clyde eyed Rand closely. "That's one reason we're counting on a good glove man at second."

"Hope I can do the job for you," said Rand, fingering his glove nervously, "but what about last year's second baseman?"

"Oh, Joe Steele. He's too old to play in our division. You've got the job all locked up."

"Gosh. How do you know?"

"You know baseball," insisted Clyde. "And besides, we only have about eight guys that want to play. In slow pitch, most teams have ten players. Heck, last year, we had to play some games with only eight."

"You said in your letter that you called yourselves the Ludell Leapers?"

"That's right. The Ludell Leapers. Pride of the West."

"Well," said Rand, noticing several pickups driving into the ball park. "If you have only eight or nine players, that's a good way to keep team morale up. Everyone gets to play."

Rand watched the boys pile out of the pickups as Clyde explained that twelve-year-old farm youths could drive to and from Ludell, providing it was on a farming errand. Fortunately for Ludell youngsters, the local sheriff was a softball fan

10

and interpreted the Kansas law to include softball as part of farming chores.

Clyde pointed toward the players. "Notice that tall guy? That's our pitcher. Willie Robbins."

Rand eyed a tall youth with long arms dangling toward the ground. Willie was bare to the waist and was hiding the ball behind his back before throwing it to a teammate. A giant scar in the shape of an upside-down **L** slashed down Willie's right arm.

"See that scar? Willie got caught in a baler when he was a baby. Broke a couple of bones and really messed him up for awhile." Clyde motioned to Rand to get out of the pickup. "He can really fool the hitters. And I think it's because he's so loose with that arm. He can hide that ball until the last moment before he pitches."

They walked through a gate in the fence to where most of the players had now gathered around home plate.

"By the way," said Clyde, joining the group. "This is my cousin from the home of the Mets." He waved toward Rand. "He's gonna give us some of that baseball know-how."

The players nodded at Rand and the new second baseman flipped his glove in a baseball greeting.

Clyde reached for a bat. "Let's have a little

"He can really fool the hitters."

fielding practice. Why don't you guys go to the positions you played last year?" He walked closer to Rand as the players ran out to the dirt infield and the brightly colored bases. "That's Tommy going to first. Matt and Patt are heading for the outfield. Dirty Mutt here is the catcher. Willie will pitch. I'll handle third and you'll be at second."

Rand jogged out to his position, but his high hopes of playing on a winning softball team were quickly fading as he looked around at his teammates. He would be playing with a pitcher who wasn't allowed to throw hard because of a rule, with two outfielders who were so small they could barely see over the outfield fence, with a left-handed first baseman who looked sleepy, a third baseman left over from a 1930's movie, and a catcher named Dirty Mutt. On top of all that, with only seven players in a game where teams normally had ten players.

The crack of the bat brought him back to the game. Clyde had hit a slow roller toward him. Rand ranged to his left, made a good stop, and whipped it to the first baseman.

"Thata baby," said Clyde, clapping his hands. "That's the old Met spirit."

Rand moved back to his normal position closer

to second base. He felt better now, after showing how he could field.

Clyde hit more grounders to the infield and a few flies to the outfield. Rand handled five or six ground balls without a bobble. He once ranged far to his right on the other side of the red base to smother a hot smash. He sprang like a cat just at the edge of the buffalo grass and with the flick of his wrist threw a chest-high peg to the first base-man.

"Maybe you ought to hit me some," said Clyde, pointing to Rand. "Then we'll have some batting practice."

Rand trotted toward home plate and Willie moved closer to watch the action before throwing for batting practice.

Rand took the ball from the catcher, grabbed a bat, and hit a slow roller to Clyde a few steps off third. Clyde charged like a mad bull, picked up the ball and in one motion fired a sidearm fastball to first base. He fell in a heap a few feet from Rand. He wiped a handful of dirt from his lips and dusted himself off.

"Well, co-manager! Need to learn how to stand up a little better." He broke out in a giant smile, showing his chipped front tooth covered with dirt. He trotted back to his position and Rand belted him a dozen more grounders. Several got through his legs when he raised up too soon on slow rollers, but Rand realized that this Clyde—this cousin, this modern Tom Sawyer—was not a softball player, or baseball player, for that matter, without ability. He might rush ground balls too fast, or throw the ball without getting set first, but he was good.

As Rand belted ground balls through the infield to the twin fleas, or hit smashes to the first baseman, or his cousin at third, he became more and more impressed with the brute skill this sandlot team possessed. Most were awkward, but there was something unusually good about the defensive skills of the Ludell Leapers.

Clyde motioned for Rand to lead off the hitting session of practice. Rand drilled the first pitch from Willie over the first baseman's head and the ball slammed against the red snow fence. He hit the next ball hard over Clyde's head at third base. Rand then hit a low knee-high pitch through the middle and slammed a down-the-middle slow pitch toward the first base line.

"Okay, new hitter up!" he yelled, jumping out of the batting cage and running to pick up his glove. He was excited at the "baseballishness" of softball—the thrill of hitting the ball, the crack

15

of the bat, the competition, that feeling running up his spine. It was the same.

Tommy motioned for Willie to throw him a pitch shoulder high on the inside of the plate. He then lashed a hit past the vacant spot at shortstop. He hit four more spot pitches through the infield and then popped out in front of the pitcher.

Clyde was up next and he belted five balls, one so far it cleared the red snow fence in center field. He smashed one toward the vacant third base, picked up his glove, and walked back to the mound to let the twin outfielders, Matt and Patt, hit.

The boys were both spray hitters. They slammed the ball anywhere they wanted, from third base to the first base line. Matt cracked a hit up the middle, and the catcher, Dirty Mutt, moved into the batter's cage.

Rand was daydreaming when suddenly someone yelled, "Look out, fella." He flopped to the ground just in time to see a bullet off the bat of the catcher rip past his head. He could hear the spinning of the ball as it raced by. The catcher ran out to make sure Rand was all right. He was still carrying his bat.

"I'm okay," said Rand, dusting himself off. "It was my own fault."

Willie poked the catcher. "Dirty Mutt, you've

got to learn to pull those outside pitches instead
of going with the pitch. See what you've done?
You nearly killed our new manager."

Rand motioned for the catcher to go back to
the plate. "Not his fault. I was dreaming about
something. Maybe I'll wake up."

Dirty Mutt hit four more balls to close out practice. Rand put his glove under his arm and joined
the rest of the team around the batting cage. The
sun was fast disappearing behind the horizon and
it was time to call a halt to the team's first practice
of the softball season.

Chapter 2

Clyde headed the battered pickup back toward his father's farm along a different road.

"I wish we had at least one more player," he said. "We've only got seven."

"I thought you said most teams have ten?" Rand asked.

Clyde nodded. "Most teams do. But finding players may be a real problem."

"Don't some more kids want to play?"

"It's not that. There just aren't many kids around here. The few not playing are too busy helping their dads in the field."

Rand shook his head and watched a grasshopper chewing on a gunny sack on the floor of the truck. Clyde pointed toward a small lake ahead of them. "Thought you might want to take a look at the local scenery before we go home. This is called Crystal Springs."

Rand was still deep in thought about softball. "What's the best you can do here?"

"Well, there's a tournament after the season's over and if you win that you get to go over to this town of Barnard to play for the state championship."

"You mean the league standings don't mean a thing?"

"League standings!" replied Clyde. "We just play a bunch of pickup games. There's not a league in this part of the country." He stopped at a clearing near an area of cattails. "Want you to see the lake here. It's really pretty at night."

Both boys climbed out and edged their way through the field of cattails and across a small dam. Clyde pointed across the water. "Over there's my dad's farm, and up there," he pointed toward a bluff on the other side of the dam, "that's where the Indian lives."

"The Indian?"

"There's this Indian who moved here. He's been raising hogs. Seems like a nice enough fella, but you don't see him much."

Rand stared toward the bluff.

"Dad says he's Kickapoo," Clyde added.

19

"He's got what?" asked Rand.

"Oh, come on. I mean he's from the Kickapoo Indian tribe. They've got a reservation not too far from here."

"Oh, the Kickapoos. I thought they came from Wisconsin," said Rand.

"They did once, but they had to move. Some went to Illinois, some came here. Some even went to Mexico."

Rand had started back to the pickup when a loud yell froze him in his tracks. "What was that?"

"Got me," said Clyde, his voice loud in the silence.

"Think it could be someone in trouble?" asked Rand.

"Don't know," replied Clyde.

The two moved over to the edge of the cattails and watched closely for movement around the lake. They scanned the shoreline, but saw nothing.

"Must have been a screech owl," said Clyde. He turned and started for the pickup. Suddenly, another loud yell pierced the air. Both boys looked back across the lake. Dark shadows raced through the tall grass and disappeared into the night.

"Good gosh!" said Clyde. "Someone must be in trouble."

Rand's heart was pumping so loudly he could

. . . **a loud yell froze him in his tracks**

barely hear his cousin.

"Maybe if we edge around this side of the lake we can see what's going on." Clyde motioned Rand to follow him. "Now, here's what we'll do," said Clyde, speaking in a whisper. "We'll sneak down there in the tall grass and if we stay behind those cottonwood trees we ought to be able to see what's going on." Rand nodded, and the two moved slowly along the edge of the tall grass. They ducked down when they heard another blood-curdling yell.

"Sounds like someone's getting killed," whispered Clyde.

"Sounds to me like we're too late," said Rand. "Why don't we leave? He's probably dead by now."

Clyde reached over and pulled Rand closer to him. "Aw, come on. It's just probably someone catching some fish or something."

"It's the something that worries me," whispered Rand. "I've never tangled with a real killer before."

"Think I have?" replied Clyde.

"Well, then, what are we doing here?"

Clyde didn't have time to answer as another screech echoed across the lake. He raised higher to see. "Come on. I think if we move quickly we can get to that tree over there." Clyde raced for a cottonwood some ten feet ahead. Rand followed so closely that when Clyde stopped, Rand ran right into him, knocking him down. Neither said a word, just jumped up quickly and fell behind the tree.

"That was close," said Rand, breathing heavily.

"You're telling me," said Clyde, wiping the perspiration off his forehead and slowly edging around the trunk to get a clearer picture of whatever was ahead. Suddenly, he turned toward Rand and sat down with his back to the tree.

"See something over yonder," he whispered. "Looks like a man chasing someone. We better make a run for it."

Clyde started running, his cousin not far behind. They raced along the edge of the lake and circled past the cattail patch and were heading back toward the pickup when something jumped out of the bushes, knocking Rand to the ground.

"Aw, got you, you little varmint," yelled the intruder. "Run away from me, will you?"

Clyde, who was some ten feet ahead of Rand, turned around at the sound. When he saw the intruder wrestling with his cousin, he charged at both figures. In his haste, he stumbled over his own feet, so instead of landing on the pair, he hurtled over them into the shallow part of the lake.

The intruder was now standing over Rand, hands on hips. "What in blazes. . . ."

Rand was leaning back on his hands. He looked up. "What's the big idea, fella?"

"What's the big idea, yourself?" came the reply. "What's the idea of chasing my pigs away?"

Clyde had managed to pull himself out of the mud and joined in the discussion. "Now, fella," he said, raising a hand, "we just heard some yelling and we came down here to help out."

The stranger moved closer to Clyde. "You wanted to help?" He motioned toward the far side of the lake. "All I was doing was chasing a pig that got out of the pen."

Rand stood up and brushed himself off. Clyde rubbed his muddy hands in the grass. The stranger took a deep breath. There was silence for several moments, and the quietness seemed to ease the tension.

"Sorry," the stranger said, sitting down suddenly. "Thought you guys were trying to steal the pig."

"Steal a pig!" said Rand, and dusted the seat of his pants again. Clyde, who was eying the stranger, motioned with his hand. "My name's Clyde Keeler. Live over yonder. What's yours?"

"They call me Leaping Frog."

Clyde rubbed the back of his neck thoughtfully. "Sort of a different name, isn't it?"

"Guess so, to a white. But for an Indian, it's all right."

"If you ask me," said Rand, walking toward the other two boys, "it's darn funny."

"Can you think of something better to go with Frog?" demanded the Indian youth. He jumped up and grabbed Rand around the neck by his shirt. "You ever wondered 'bout your stupid name?"

Clyde mover closer hurriedly. "What Rand here means, it just doesn't sound like Smith or Jones, or something like that. He ain't used to hearing, you might say, names that are earthy—that's it, downright earthy, like Leaping Frog." He looked toward the sky. "You know, you say that word a couple of times and it has a ring to it. Yeah. Leaping Frog. Downright earthy sound to it. Don't you think, Rand?"

Rand couldn't answer. Leaping Frog still had his hand around his neck. Rand managed to work himself free and stepped back. "Yeah," he stammered, "name's not bad. Just unusual."

The Indian youth was still unhappy. "You saying it's a funny name?" He stepped forward. "You're calling Frog a funny name?" He reached over and choked Rand around the neck again.

Clyde started to interfere but, noticing the strength in the Indian's arms, stopped suddenly. "You know, I think most anyone would go for an earthy name like Frog. It's got that ring to it, like Fish or Bass. Gosh! You could be called most anything. With a name like Frog, it doesn't really matter. Leaping Frog is a good old country name." He turned and looked at Rand, whose face was turning a bright red. "In fact, the more I think about it, the more I wish my name was Frog. Don't you, Rand?"

Having freed himself again from Leaping Frog, Rand slowly straightened his shirt. "Yeah, Leaping Frog's a great name." He then caught a breath of air, raised on his tiptoes, and pushed himself toward the Indian. "Like Hop Toad or Horny Lizard!"

"Why you little mouth," yelled Leaping Frog. He reached over and with both hands pushed Rand to the ground. "I ought to break your big nose. And I would if you were half man-size instead of being a little mousy half-pint. You . . . you . . . Uncle Tomahawk!"

Clyde stepped between the fallen Rand and the enraged Indian. He looked to make sure Rand was still on the ground and then put his hand on the Indian's shoulder. "He doesn't mean any harm," said Clyde, turning Leaping Frog around. "He's no country boy like us, but he don't mean no harm. He's just a little keyed up from his long trip from the East today. Yes, sir, still keyed up from his long trip. Isn't that right, Rand?"

Rand didn't answer, but he remained seated. He couldn't get a clear picture of Leaping Frog in the dark but he didn't need a bright sun to tell that the Indian was not only strong but big as well. His hands, pressed against Rand's neck, had felt like giant hammers.

Even in the dark, muscles seemed to swell Leaping Frog's clothes. His waist gave way to a large chest and he looked as if he had been formed by someone holding his middle and squeezing.

By now, minutes after the pushing contest, Rand had gotten over his temper fit and Leaping Frog seemed in a better frame of mind as well. The boys were eying each other closely when a small pig darted from behind Leaping Frog and Clyde toward Rand, who was still sitting on the ground. Quick as a wink, Leaping Frog moved. The pig squealed as the Indian scooped up the animal in one quick, graceful motion. "Got you," he said, grabbing the pig by the snoot. "You're not going to get away this time."

Rand had fallen back, but amazingly Leaping Frog hadn't even touched him despite the fact that the pig was only a short distance from him.

"Say," said Rand, noticing the quick hands of Leaping Frog. "You ever played softball?"

"Softball? Naw," said Leaping Frog, trying to keep the pig from squealing. "Didn't have a team on the reservation where I lived."

"That thing sitting is Rand Cogburn," said Clyde suddenly. He walked closer to the Indian and the squealing pig. "Where did you say you're from?"

"From up north on a reservation." He motioned with his head toward the house on the bluff. "Came down here to help my uncle with the pigs this summer."

The squealing porker almost jumped out of Leaping Frog's arms, but the Indian grabbed him firmly. "Better be going. This pig is ready to be let loose."

When Leaping Frog started walking toward his uncle's house, Clyde followed.

"Hope you're not sore about the misunderstanding?"

"Naw, forget it."

"Well, then," called Rand, "how about playing on our softball team?"

"You guys want *me* on your team?" Leaping Frog shook his head in amazement. "I've never even *seen* a softball game."

"You'll learn fast," replied Rand quickly, jumping up. "Why, it's as easy as scooping up that pig. What do you say? It's a lot of fun. And another thing. Clyde and I will pick you up for practice at six-thirty on Tuesdays and Thursdays. Will you play?"

Leaping Frog kept walking through the tall grass toward a dike pathway that led to the house. Rand stopped as the tall figure disappeared into the darkness and yelled one final time, "See you at practice this Thursday?"

There were a few seconds of silence mixing around the sounds of water splashing on shore. Suddenly, like an arrow piercing the night air, Leaping Frog's answer came whistling through the trees. "I'll come."

Rand grinned from ear to ear and ran after Clyde toward the pickup.

Chapter 3

Rand and Clyde spent most of the following days in the hayfield throwing bales onto the back of a flat-bed trailer and then unloading them onto a giant haystack at the end of the field. They loaded and stacked over sixteen hundred bales before they quit on Tuesday evening for practice.

They gassed the pickup and headed toward the softball diamond by way of the Indian's house. Leaping Frog sat by the mailbox at the edge of the main road. Clyde honked the horn. "Hop aboard."

Leaping Frog jumped into the back of the pickup and Rand turned to look at him closely through the cab's rear window. It was the first time he had seen the youth in daylight. Leaping Frog's hair was cropped in an early Beatle cut, with half his ears showing. The skin stretched taut and coppery over his cheekbones and his black eyes were wide and deep.

The trio remained silent until Leaping Frog yelled, "Nice hot evening. Isn't it?"

"Like a dog day," Clyde yelled back.

The wind was blowing Leaping Frog's hair and he pushed it out of his eyes. No one said any more until they pulled in at the softball diamond. The rest of the team had already arrived.

"Say, fellas, I want you to meet a new member of the team," said Clyde, slamming the pickup door. "This is Leaping Frog. He's staying with the Indian for the summer and wants to play with us."

The players said "hello" or "hey" or "nice to have you on the team." Rand had gone out toward second base and was picking up loose pieces of dirt when he heard Clyde tell Leaping Frog to play shortstop. Leaping Frog hustled out beside him.

"Don't you use a glove?" asked Rand, disapprovingly. "You can't catch hot grounders with your bare hands."

Leaping Frog motioned to Clyde to hit the ball toward him. Rand was picking up another loose clod of dirt when he heard the crack of the bat. He looked up to see Leaping Frog move quickly to his right, reach down with one bare hand, and flip the ball sidearm to first.

"You should use both hands," said Rand.

"You catch 'em your way and I'll catch 'em mine," Leaping Frog replied. "I'll have better luck with my bare hands than you'll have with that cowhide covering yours."

When Clyde belted a hot smash to the left of Rand, the New York second baseman took two short steps toward the base and, as the ball started to scoop past him, threw himself toward it. The ball hit the webbing of his glove with a thud and rolled slowly toward the red base. Rand jumped up quickly and rifled a perfect strike to the first baseman. He dusted off his pants, pulled at his belt, and eyed Leaping Frog, feeling as if he'd won a war against the Indians. Leaping Frog seemed unconcerned. He motioned toward Clyde and the redhead hit a clothesline drive to the right of the Indian. With the speed of a streaking arrow, Leaping Frog raced toward the ball, leaped at the last moment, and pulled the ball down with one hand. He then flipped a soft peg to Rand at second. Rand watched the ball fall beside him, then slowly picked it up and tossed it toward Clyde at home plate.

"We're getting the runner at first now," said

Rand, looking at Leaping Frog. "There's no room for show-offs on this team."

Leaping Frog didn't answer and walked toward the baby blue of third base.

The rest of the fielding session went smoothly and Leaping Frog overcame some of his shyness brought about by the conflict with Rand. Batting practice followed and went well, except Leaping Frog failed to hit the ball out of the infield. After watching the Indian slash wildly at several pitches, Rand called a halt to practice.

The three climbed into the front seat of the old pickup and headed home. Clyde and Leaping Frog were discussing how beautiful the night was when they pulled up to the Indian's farm.

"See you next practice," said Clyde, opening the door to let Leaping Frog out. Rand looked straight ahead and smashed his fist into the pocket of his glove. Leaping Frog slid across the truck seat and stepped to the ground. Clyde nudged Leaping Frog. "We'll stop for you Thursday."

Leaping Frog nodded and walked toward the house.

"You're being a little hard on Leaping Frog, don't you think?" said Clyde, sliding into the pickup.

Rand shook his head. "He's got to learn to hit

if he's going to help the team. That Indian's got to learn to hit."

"Yeah, but he's a good fielder," said Clyde, turning a sharp corner. "This was his first practice, and remember, he never played softball before." He nudged Rand with his elbow. "His hitting will get better."

Rand wasn't as convinced as Clyde that their eighth ballplayer was going to make the Ludell Leapers the best softball team in the country. A picture of Leaping Frog slashing wildly at the ball kept flashing into his mind.

"You've got to remember, he didn't hit one ball out of the infield," said Rand. "Why did I have to go and ask him to play when I knew he had never even played before?"

"Come on," said Clyde. "A manager can help a good player like that, Rand. You can work with him extra in batting practice. He's going to help our team, I'll bet on it."

Chapter 4

Twice a week the Ludell Leapers practiced softball, and Leaping Frog was fielding nicely. It was
amazing how well the Indian could move around
the diamond. He was like a ballet dancer with an
arm like a rocket. He could charge in on a ground
ball, scoop it up like Brooks Robinson, and fire to
first in time to get the runner. He still refused to
wear a glove, insisting he could depend more on
his hands.

In the meanwhile, Rand learned one thing about
slow-pitch softball played in the Sunflower State
that he didn't like. There were no definite rules, or
at least none at the level of the Ludell Leapers.
He had been in the habit of going over baseball
rules with his friends in New York, and whenever
something happened in a game that needed defin-

ing, it was easily found in the rule book. But here, whenever a disagreement arose, the final decision was simply made by the umpire.

The relationship between Clyde and Leaping Frog continued friendly, but Rand and Leaping Frog had conflicts, and it all centered around baseball, or rather, slow-pitch softball. Rand was especially upset because Leaping Frog seemed unconcerned about what Rand called "baseball's basic rules," which he tried to redirect to softball. Rand's rules included hitting behind the runner, knowing when to slide or go into a base standing up, and how many bases to take on a ground ball hit through the infield—all fundamentals a baseball fanatic like Rand took for granted.

Leaping Frog did everything from instinct, except hit. Sometimes this presented a problem not only to Rand but to the team.

In the first game with Deerfield, the first three innings went smoothly with Leaping Frog handling five ground balls cleanly. But at the plate, he didn't lift the bat off his shoulder and watched a third strike go by.

Deerfield got a base hit in the bottom of the fourth and, with one out, the batter hit a smash to Rand at second base. He flipped to Leaping Frog, covering the bag. The runner was barreling to-

ward second and came in sliding high at Leaping
Frog in an attempt to stop the double play. Leaping Frog was dumped violently to the ground but
held onto the ball for the force out. He dusted himself off, and suddenly jumped at the surprised runner with both feet.

"What are you doing?" yelled Rand.

"Gonna teach him a lesson," the Indian replied,
his knees resting on the runner's throat. "He ought
to know better than to come sliding in at *me* like
that."

Clyde ran over from third base. The runner's
face was completely red and his Adam's apple was
bobbing like a cork on a fisherman's line. His
teammates dashed onto the field. Clyde grabbed
Leaping Frog away from several angry players.

"Hold it," he yelled, pulling the red-faced vis-
itor to his feet. "Everything's okay here. Just a
little misunderstanding."

The on-rushing Deerfield players had stopped
short of Clyde, noticing his big arms and the ease
with which he had picked up their teammate.

"Well," said one, "let's don't get sore over a little slide."

Leaping Frog edged toward the player, and
Clyde grabbed his shirt. "The slide was too high,
but we're here to play ball. We're not going to

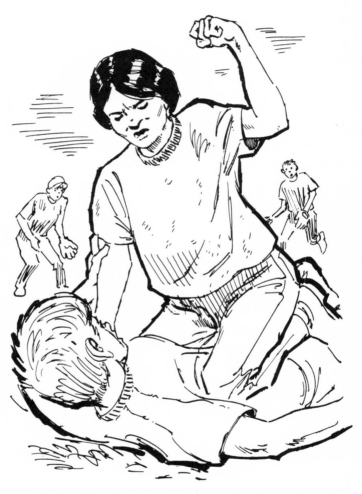

"Gonna teach him a lesson," the Indian replied.

fight over a little ball game or a high slide. We're here to have fun, not fight." Several of the players grumbled, but it seemed no one wanted to tangle with the muscle man or the enraged Indian.

Rand was still standing beside second base. His heart was pounding like a mad bongo player, and he had to admit he admired Leaping Frog's spunk. He patted Leaping Frog on the back as he passed. The Deerfield players returned to their side of the field, the red-faced runner limping along behind. Willie forced the next hitter to pop out to Clyde for the last out of the inning.

In the top of the fifth, Leaping Frog was the first hitter. He watched two pitches go by for balls and then hit the dirt as a high lob pitch almost beaned him on top of the head. He dusted his dirty jeans off and took his stance in the batter's box. On the next pitch, Leaping Frog swung as hard as he could, and the bat went flying out of his hands several feet past the pitcher's head.

"Throwing at a guy is about as bad as sliding hard into him," yelled Leaping Frog. "You want to play silly games? I'll play your silly games."

Clyde stormed from the bench toward the mound and waved his arms so everyone could see. "Now, you fellas, listen good. We're going to play ball without any fighting or I'm going to take things in my own hands." He pushed back the sleeve of his sweat shirt and waved toward the Deerfield players. Rand sat still at the edge of the bench. He was amazed at the spunk Leaping Frog was showing. He slowly stood up and walked toward Leaping Frog at home plate.

"Way to stand your ground. That's another one of those baseball rules you don't want to forget."

Clyde walked off the field and Leaping Frog stepped back into the box. The pitcher threw the next pitch and Leaping Frog hit a weak grounder to the third baseman who threw him out by ten feet.

The rest of the game went by smoothly. Deerfield scored one more run but Ludell scored five, one on a triple by Clyde after Rand had opened the inning with a solid single through the middle. The team played a great game defensively. The twins played flawlessly and Willie had good control. After he had seen the batters once and sized their strength and weaknesses, he had them hitting the ball to the infield or hitting high fly balls to Matt and Patt in the outfield. The game ended with the Leapers clearly in command, 5-2, and they had their first win of the season.

On the way home Rand was as excited as if he'd just heard the Mets had won a doubleheader over the Pirates. Clyde was his usual self, talking first about softball, then about the wheat ripening in the fields.

Leaping Frog was quiet. He talked some about the Indian's wheat, the beauty of the night, but very little about the game. Rand, whose mind never left the subject of baseball, or now softball, broke the silence.

"You fielded like a real champ tonight," he said, turning to look at Leaping Frog who was sitting beside him.

"Yeah," said Clyde, joining the conversation. "I've never seen a guy catch so many balls without a glove."

Leaping Frog nodded. "Yeah, but I can't hit the ball."

"I know," said Rand, "but we'll help you. You're not meeting the ball. You need to level off your swing and try to hit the ball where it's pitched."

"I don't know," said Leaping Frog. "I don't seem to get the hang of it. Maybe I ought to forget about softball."

Rand looked nervously at Clyde in the darkness. Clyde reached over and patted Leaping Frog on the knee. "Aw, it's a lot of fun. Just don't take the game so seriously."

"We need every player we can get," said Rand, "no matter how bad a hitter he is. I mean, a couple more practices and you'll be hitting like Clyde."

"Oh, it's not only the hitting that bothers me. It's a lot of other things. Important things."

Clyde shifted into second as they started up a hill. "What other things?"

"Oh, a lot of things besides softball," the Indian said, leaning back in the seat. "Like you don't even know my uncle's name."

"Well, he's only lived beside us a couple months," said Clyde, rather defensively. He blinked his lights at an oncoming car. "Besides, I wave at him every time I see him."

"But you still don't know his name," said Leaping Frog. "Well, his name is Tom. Tom Frog."

The cousins were silent. "You know why my folks named me Leaping?" The Kickapoo answered his own question. "Because they wanted me to have an Indian name. A name an Indian would want to have. Tom's not an Indian name."

Clyde and Rand were unprepared for such a change in the conversation. But Leaping Frog seemed more interested in talking about his background than the softball victory. It was as if someone had unplugged the hole in a bathtub.

"I've been doing a lot of reading about Indians

in the paper. You know, I can still hear my teacher at the reservation. She would say, 'The worst thing to be in this country is a native American. The American Indian doesn't live like an American citizen. He's not governed by the government. Most of the Indians still live on the same reservations set up by the white man who took away their land.' "

"I've been reading about Indians, too," said Clyde. "I guess there're still having problems. And there's a lot in the papers about women. Why, I saw yesterday that a Little League team disbanded just because a girl wanted to play on the team!"

Leaping Frog turned to stare at him. "Indians. Yes, and women, too," he said thoughtfully.

The boys sat silent a moment. Then, Leaping Frog suddenly brightened as the edge of the moon appeared over a bluff.

"Hey, that's a full moon," said Leaping Frog.

"So?" said Rand, eyeing the sky.

"It's time for the Trip to the Frogs!"

"Trip to the Frogs?" asked Clyde.

"Sure," said Leaping Frog, getting excited, "and Crystal Springs is nearby. We can go there."

"Why?"

"To play an Indian game."

Clyde and Rand looked at each other strangely.

43

"Tell you what I'll do," said Leaping Frog. "If you'll play my Indian game tonight, I'll play your game of softball all summer. Okay?"

Clyde grinned at Leaping Frog, and at Rand, who was staring at his Indian friend.

"Come on," said Leaping Frog, poking at Rand. "Everybody knows the white man's games like softball, but nobody knows about our games. Come on," he pleaded. "It doesn't take long to learn."

Rand drove his fist into his glove. "Sure, why not?" he said, smiling at Leaping Frog. "You play softball and we'll play your Indian game."

Clyde turned the lights on bright and headed toward Crystal Springs. "Okay, Leaping Frog. You're on. Time for the Trip to the Frogs!"

Chapter 5

The moon had gone behind the clouds by the time the trio arrived at Crystal Springs. Leaping Frog explained that, according to Indian custom, the Trip to the Frogs was held yearly for those who had reached their twelfth birthday. It was a type of initiation designed to show who had the most determination, who was the strongest swimmer, who was destined to be a leader in the tribe, and the future of the tribe.

The swimmers spent months practicing underwater with a bullfrog strapped to their sides to prepare for the summer contest, learning to hold their breaths for long periods of time. In earlier days, the swimmers were greased with hog lard and taken to a giant log in the middle of the lake. Later they were clad in suits made of deerskin, each suit with a holster for the frog. The bullfrogs were symbols of underwater prowess and, after the contest, were eaten at a giant frog-leg feast. If all the swimmers made it to shore, it was an omen that the tribe would live in peace.

Leaping Frog led the three toward the spot where they had first met with the pig. Motioning for the others to wait, he edged toward the water over a muddy area filled with pig and cow tracks. He reached down with the same speed he used to gobble up hard-hit ground balls and lifted a long-legged bullfrog from the water.

He motioned with his head toward a clearing where the water slapped evenly on the shore. The trio waded through the tall grass along the water's edge and past cottonwood trees until they reached the area.

"This is it," said Leaping Frog, pointing toward the water. "I've practiced here sometimes while I was waiting for a full moon." He looked at Clyde and Rand. "Either one of you guys have a belt?"

The boys shook their heads.

"We need something to hold the frog," said Leaping Frog. There was silence, except for the wind rustling the cottonwood leaves.

"Got it," yelled Leaping Frog, so loudly that the frog almost jumped out of his hands. "We can

46

use that old glove of yours. It's a three-fingered glove and it'd work perfectly." He pointed the frog at Rand.

"Use my *glove?*"

"Sure, Rand. You said the other day that it was an old glove, and a little water's not going to hurt it."

Rand couldn't help but wonder if Tom Seaver had ever jumped into a pond with a frog in a baseball glove. It didn't seem likely.

"Come on. What do you say, Rand?"

Rand shrugged his shoulders. "I don't really care, I guess."

"Great," said Leaping Frog. "I'll get the glove from the pickup." He handed the frog to Rand and ran toward the road.

Rand looked at the large frog moving uneasily in his grip. He cocked an uneasy eye at Clyde standing with his hands in his back pockets. A half smile seemed frozen on his face.

The pair remained still, fanned by the mild Kansas breeze, until they heard Leaping Frog threshing through the weeds. The Indian stumbled over to Rand, who quickly pushed the frog toward him. Leaping Frog carefully nuzzled the frog headfirst into the large part of the glove.

"Now if we're careful, we can put our thumbs

in the glove and our hands around the frog. When we swim we'll just have to shorten our breast stroke motion a bit."

Leaping Frog walked to the edge of the lake. "Okay, you better take your shoes off, **Rand**. New Yorkers are always first!"

Rand frowned at the water, inches away. He walked past Leaping Frog, past Clyde standing with his arms folded, and into the lake. He jumped out quickly.

"Oh, one more thing. It would be easier to swim without your shirt. You can leave your jeans on."

Leaping Frog moved toward Rand with the frog-filled glove and gently nudged him. "Since we don't want anyone to drown, we'll change the rules some. Why don't you get in the water here where it's shallow, and swim along the edge of the bank to that big tree?" He pointed to a giant cottonwood some twenty-five feet away. "And remember, Rand, blow bubbles as you swim so we can follow you. Swim until you're tired and then come up for more air. The water is not deep so you can stand up anywhere." He handed the frog-glove to Rand.

Rand molded his hand around the frog and moved slowly into the water. It got colder as it reached his knees and slapped against his body.

48

The glove was underwater, and Rand could feel the frog kicking against his hand.

He took a deep breath and submerged. Water pressure pushed against his ears as he sank deeper. He kicked forward, blowing bubbles as he glided along. He moved his right arm boldly, but stroked gently with the hand holding the frog, which was now kicking violently in the glove. The murky water forced him to close his eyes tightly.

A thousand thoughts raced through his mind. A picture of Tom Seaver kept popping into it. As he kicked, it seemed as if he were Seaver, pitching and reaching back and kicking extra hard to throw a third strike to win the pennant for the Mets. His head started to hurt from lack of oxygen and his chest seemed ready to explode. He kicked extra hard, sensing that the spot where he was to surface was near. He suddenly rubbed against a tree branch in the mud. He stopped swimming and pushed violently out of the water, lifting the frog and glove victoriously over his head.

"Thata baby," yelled Leaping Frog, who was standing ten feet away. He and Clyde had followed the underwater swimmer along the shore. "You've just become a Kickapoo warrior!"

Rand slowly waded toward the pair, carrying the frog still nuzzled in the glove. He handed the glove to Leaping Frog, and threw himself on the bank. "I'll say this for you Indians," he gasped. "You don't play easy games."

The moon had slipped from behind a cloud and was shining through the trees, brightening the lake shore. Rand regained his breath quickly. He watched the Indian take the frog out of the glove to see how it had endured the underwater swim. The frog seemed relaxed and made no attempt to jump for freedom.

"You ready, Clyde?"

Clyde unfolded his arms and led the trio back to the opposite side of the lake. He wasted little time removing his sweat shirt and shoes, and put on the glove. He stepped quickly into the water and dived headfirst, splashing water back to shore. Shortly, giant bubbles could be seen in the little waves. The trail moved swiftly toward the tree.

The pair followed the bubbles from the shoreline. The water swirled every time the Kansas farm boy took a stroke only inches below the surface. Clyde was pulling himself closer to the tree with every movement. He swam much as he played softball—with a great deal of strength and ability, but with little finesse. As he hit the large branch, he pulled himself up and raised the frog and glove high above his head. He grinned up at Leaping

Frog. "How did I do, Big Chief?"

"In our tribe," said Leaping Frog, taking the glove and frog from Clyde, "you'd rank as a warrior."

The wind had increased in velocity and a large cloud was now blocking the moon's view of the Trip to the Frogs. The lights had gone out at the Indian's house above the lake. The leaves rustling and the water splashing against the bank were the only sounds to be heard. Leaping Frog led the way back to the starting spot. He suddenly became very quiet and seemed reluctant to get started. He inspected the frog for a second time and was placing it back in the three-fingered glove when Clyde broke the silence.

"You about ready?"

Leaping Frog sat down in the grass, removed his shoes, and paused, looking across the water.

"You know, I've been thinking. Some Indians have a choice in the Trip to the Frogs. The rules are different for . . . for some."

"What do you mean?" asked Rand.

"Well, the . . . some of the . . . better swimmers could get into the water at . . . er . . . er . . ." He stuttered a bit and finished in a rush. "Say at their favorite spot."

"Can't you just pick out your favorite spot

now?" asked Clyde.

"I mean, when no one's looking. It's more of a test of swimming ability if no one sees you enter the water or knows where you are."

"Then what do you want us to do?" asked Rand. "It's getting darn cold out here and we're all wet."

"I'd like you to go behind that tree and turn your backs."

The boys were puzzled, but walked over and stood behind the tree. In several seconds, they heard Leaping Frog splash into the water. They turned and ran toward the lake.

"Did you see where he went in?" asked Rand.

"No, but he should come out about the same place we did."

They scanned the surface of the water for bubbles, but the darkness made it difficult to see. The minutes flew by with still no sign of Leaping Frog.

"Let's walk back to the spot where we came out," said Clyde. Rand nodded and the two carefully followed the water's edge back toward the cottonwood where the pair had finished their Trips to the Frogs. But there was still no sign of the Indian.

"We had better do something quick. I'm afraid he'll drown," said Rand.

The boys rushed along the lake, scanning the shoreline. Suddenly, Rand stopped. "Look, Clyde!"

The pair stared at a pile of clothing, stacked neatly a few inches from the water. A pair of jeans covered a sweat shirt and undergarments.

"For some reason he took off more than his sweat shirt," said Rand. "Don't Indians swim with clothes on?"

"You've got me, but I suppose you can swim better naked. And the ancient Indians only wore hog lard. Do you think . . ." A piercing yell interrupted Clyde's question.

They could see a silhouette on the other side of the lake.

The wind and the water lapping onto shore made it difficult to hear.

"Do you think that's Leaping Frog?" asked Rand.

"It must be. No one else in his right mind would be out here."

The boys listened closely as another cry echoed across the lake.

"Sounds like Leaping Frog," said Clyde, "but I can't be sure."

The wind stilled momentarily and it was easier to hear. "This is Leaping Frog," came a clear voice

"Do you think that's Leaping Frog?" asked Rand.

across the water. "Decided to swim across the lake. It's a tougher game. Only for Kickapoos! 'Bye, see you at softball practice."

The boys watched the silhouette edge up the hill and disappear into the darkness of the night. Rand and Clyde turned and started walking toward the pickup in silence. The croak of a bullfrog ended their first Trip to the Frogs at Crystal Springs.

Chapter 6

It had been five days since the Trip to the Frogs and there had been no further contact between the cousins and the Indian. Rand was especially pleased this Tuesday night as they rode to practice. He had spoken to his parents by telephone for nearly half an hour. He wouldn't admit it, but it had been good to hear their voices. His mother got on one phone and his father on the extension and they had talked about everything from air pollution in New York to a new shirt his mother was sewing for him. His beloved Mets had also won an afternoon game and were riding a five-game winning streak. Tom Seaver had struck out twelve on the way to a six-hit shutout and it looked as if he was on his way to winning twenty games.

The pickup rounded the bend near the mailbox

where Leaping Frog always waited for them. The boys were relieved to see him sitting at the edge of the road pounding his fist into a glove. He was wearing the usual jeans and over-sized dark sweat shirt. The pickup rolled to a stop, and Leaping Frog jumped into the cab beside Rand. He poked the second baseman in the ribs and handed him the glove.

"Dried it, oiled it a couple times, and tied it up, molded around a softball," he said proudly. "The underwater swim didn't hurt it at all."

Rand put the glove on, and it didn't seem any worse for the wear. It was a little heavier, but the pocket was greatly expanded. "I see *you* aren't any worse from the swim." He pounded a fist into the pocket. "And I see you decided to pick up your sweat shirt, among other things." He eyed Clyde closely. The Kansan turned briefly and winked at his cousin.

"You know," said Leaping Frog, "that's the best and biggest Trip to the Frogs ever. Made it across in two breaths. Swimming underwater is the mark of a great swimmer, and there's no better place to test yourself than at Crystal Springs."

"You had us worried," said Clyde. "You made such a big deal about *us* being careful, and then *you* just took off without telling us what you were going to do."

"Well," said Leaping Frog, pushing his hair from his face. "It—it was one of those things you do on a second thought."

Rand was still testing his glove. "You got this thing about swimming without clothes?" He pounded extra hard into the pocket.

"What do you mean saying, 'You got this thing about swimming without clothes?' "

"Just what I said," replied Rand in a typical Howard Cosell style. "You left your clothes piled up near the water and, apparently, swam nude across the lake—making sure nobody saw you."

"So what?" said Leaping Frog. "It's hard to swim a long distance, especially with a frog in a glove. A sweat shirt and jeans would have made it impossible. And besides, you know it's not right for you guys to see me without any clothes." He pushed at Rand. "You know, you've got some weird notions about life, and seeing people nude."

Rand didn't answer. He was somewhat puzzled at Leaping Frog's modesty. All boys were accustomed to taking at least their shirts off in front of other boys. Apparently, Indians have some different ideas, thought Rand, and maybe Kickapoos always swim without clothes.

"Looks like all the players are here," said Clyde

as they reached the field. "We've got to be ready for the game Tuesday with Atwood. Big game." He parked the pickup directly behind home plate.

Leaping Frog jumped out and started catching with Tommy, the first sacker. Rand and Clyde brought out the bats, and Willie grabbed one and motioned for the players to take their positions.

Rand was eager to see how the remolded glove performed in the field, and he didn't have to wait long. Willie hit a hard grounder between first and second. Tommy stepped aside as Rand streaked toward the ball with the same reckless abandon that he had used to tackle the underwater swim. He ranged far to his left toward the buffalo grass of the outfield. He waited until the last moment and then dove for the ball.

The force with which the ball hit tore the glove off and sent Rand sprawling in the dry grass. He scrambled to his feet, picked up the ball, and raced a few steps to first base to make an unassisted play. He then arched the ball to Dirty Mutt at home. Rand was pleased. He knew he wouldn't have been able to stop the ball with the old glove. Leaping Frog's remolding job could make the difference in winning or losing.

Rand couldn't help but feel pleased also about the progress of the Ludell Leapers, despite their having only eight players. The fielding was flaw-less. There hadn't been a mistake or a bad throw during the entire infield practice.

Rand was still feeling pleased throughout bat-ting practice as everyone hit the ball. Clyde was the next-to-last hitter and he promptly knocked two over the fence. He sent a line drive past third and then ran out to field for the next hitter.

Leaping Frog walked slowly to the plate. He picked up the black bat Clyde had used and stepped into the batter's box. At the first pitch, a letter-high lob ball, Leaping Frog swung under the ball, spun around and fell in a heap. He had missed the ball by three feet.

"Level out your swing," yelled Rand. His feel-ing of grandeur suddenly sank. "Swing level. You can't hit the ball swinging under it two miles."

Rand trotted in from second, took the bat from Leaping Frog, and made a level swing. He pointed out the importance of keeping the back elbow level and keeping an eye on the ball. Leaping Frog listened closely, took a couple of practice swings, and stepped back in the box.

Willie tossed a knee-high inside pitch. Leaping Frog uncoiled like a rattlesnake and lashed a line drive at Clyde's head at third. He didn't have time to get his glove in front of the eye-level streaking ball, so he threw himself face down to the ground. The ball was still gaining speed when it smoked past Matt in the outfield and smashed against the snow fence. Clyde dusted the dirt from his face.

"Tell Leaping Frog to hit the ball somewhere else. A guy could get killed trying to field a blue darter like that!"

Rand wasn't that easily convinced he had solved Leaping Frog's hitting problem. He motioned for Willie to throw the same knee-high lob pitch. Willie went into his loose-goosey windup and uncorked an unusually high lob. The ball seemed to stop in mid-air as it slowly arched toward Leaping Frog's knees. The Indian waited patiently for the ball to come down and he then took a long step and swung with all of his might. The ball screamed off the bat toward Clyde at third, followed by the bat.

Leaping Frog had swung so hard that the bat slipped out of his grip and beat its way toward Clyde at the same time as the ball. Clyde's eyes got as big as saucers and he somehow managed to stick the glove in front of his face as the ball hit leather. At the same time the ball smacked into the glove, Clyde hopped over the bat. He landed in a heap on top of the blue third base.

He lay there for a moment, looking as if he thought Leaping Frog was seeking revenge for all

The ball screamed off the bat toward Clyde at third

the wrongs white people had done to the Indians. He slowly stood up.

"Trying to catch the ball's bad enough," he said, "without a bat flying at your feet at the same time. Hang onto the bat, will you, fella?" He moved back fifteen feet so he was standing almost on the outfield grass.

Rand motioned for Willie to throw Leaping Frog a chest-high strike. The next pitch sailed to the plate and Leaping Frog swung just as hard, but this time missed the ball by three feet. Rand motioned for Willie to throw only letter-high pitches, and Leaping Frog missed the ball again by a wide margin, and the next one, and the next one.

Rand instructed Leaping Frog to level off his swing, but it was such an unfamiliar motion for the Indian that his swing did not improve. No matter where the ball was pitched about the knees, Leaping Frog swung in an arching motion as if he were playing golf. Once, on a waist-high pitch, he hit the ball weakly to third, but by the time it reached Clyde it had stopped rolling.

After ten minutes of swinging and missing, and after the players in the outfield had sat down, practice was called.

"Sorry," said Leaping Frog on the way home,

"but I guess cutting weeds all my life on the reservation has hurt my swing."

Rand was still determined. "We'll just have to work on the high ones and hope Atwood pitchers Thursday won't notice you can't hit anything above your knees."

The old pickup rattled across the Kansas prairie, away from the softball diamond. Leaping Frog eyed Clyde and Rand for a long moment. The sound of a lonely coyote baying at the moon broke the silence.

Chapter 7

Rand called it a beautiful night for softball, but then he would have called any night or day a perfect time to play. The day had been windy, and dark clouds chased the evening sun to bed early. Dust was in the air, and the wind threw tumbleweeds across the sagebrush pastureland around the Ludell softball diamond. It rustled the trees, making a howling noise.

Both teams appeared on time, but the menacing weather kept most of the fans away. The teams had taken their pre-game practice and were anxious to get the game underway before the storm hit. According to Clyde, who was more of a weather prognosticator than Rand and the other players, thunderheads were forming at least thirty miles away. He looked more concerned about the strange clouds forming directly behind center field, but he didn't say anything.

Willie took the mound and lobbed three pitches over the plate and motioned to the umpire that he was ready. The first batter stepped in and promptly slammed the first pitch to Rand at second. Rand scooped it up and tossed it to Tommy for an easy out. The next hitter laced the ball past Clyde, playing in close at third, but Leaping Frog raced over, speared the ball with his throwing hand, and, in one quick motion, fired to first base to get the runner by two steps. The next hitter lofted a high fly to Matt in center field and Atwood was quickly down in order in the top of the first.

The Ludell Leapers scored a run in the bottom of the first as Clyde banged out a double, scoring Rand who had gotten a base hit and was then moved to second by Matt. The score remained 1-0 through four quick innings.

Leaping Frog was hitting eighth and in his first time at bat had swung at three pitches to go down on strikes. He was to lead off the fifth inning and, as he moved toward the plate to hit, Rand pulled him aside.

"Take every pitch that looks high to you and make him throw you one low. He doesn't have the control Willie has, so he'll throw you a low one sooner or later. Just wait in there and don't swing, unless it's a low one, and then hit the cover off it."

Leaping Frog stepped into the batter's box. He raised the bat off his shoulder and waited. The Atwood pitcher lobbed a chest-high pitch for a strike, but Leaping Frog, following Rand's advice, took the pitch. The count had run to two and two when the Atwood pitcher threw his first low pitch. It was an inside spinning ball, but Leaping Frog was ready.

He waited patiently for the ball to descend. A split second before the umpire yelled strike three, the bat of Leaping Frog slashed forward. The ball screamed off the wood and raced toward the third baseman, who threw his hands in front of his face. The ball missed his left ear by inches and streaked toward the red snow fence, and past the outfielder.

Leaping Frog raced around the bases for an inside-the-park home run to give Ludell a 2-0 lead.

Atwood came back to score two runs in the top half of the next inning, tying the game. Their catcher had swung late on one of Willie's spinning lob pitches and poked it over first base, away from the twin fly hawks who were playing the hitter to pull the ball. Tommy, the first sacker, had to chase the ball down and, by the time he got it into the infield, two runs raced home.

The score remained deadlocked at 2-2, but the Ludell Leapers threatened to break the game wide open in the bottom half of the inning. Matt belted an inside pitch past the third baseman and raced into second with a double. Dirty Mutt worked the Atwood pitcher for one of the infrequent walks in slow-pitch softball. Patt then lined out to the shortstop for the first out. Clyde hit a hard line drive over the second baseman's head and the ball headed for the fence. But the rover, or the fourth outfielder, made a leap for the ball and somehow captured it in flight. He rolled over and made a perfect throw into the infield to double Matt, sliding back into second.

Clyde walked slowly to his position at third and pointed out to Rand the black clouds that were filling in overhead. Rand motioned for Willie to begin the next inning quickly.

The Atwood shortstop hit under the first pitch, and drove it toward Leaping Frog at short. Leaping Frog had trouble following the ball in the darkness of the clouds, but managed to catch it with both hands. The next two hitters swung on the first pitches, popping up to the infield, and the game, still tied, quickly moved into the bottom half of the seventh inning.

By now, everyone seemed to be aware of the

menace directly overhead. Thunderheads had taken a back seat to mountains upon mountains of black, greenish clouds rising high above the Kansas plains. The velocity of the wind had diminished and the night was still—frightfully still. There seemed to be a strange smell in the air, as if Mother Nature were warning of an upcoming danger. The few spectators, except for some parents, had departed, but Rand insisted the game be completed.

Leaping Frog moved quickly toward the plate to lead off the bottom of the seventh. In his eagerness to pitch, the Atwood hurler neglected to keep the ball high and away from Leaping Frog's uppercut. The Indian's eyes seemed to light up like neon signs as he watched the pitch coming down toward the plate. He waited and then, with all his might, swung at the ball. In the stillness of the night, the crack of the bat meeting the ball seemed to echo across the plains. Because of the impact, no one seemed to move as the ball arched high into the clouds far down the left-field line. The outfielder turned to watch the fleeting ball go over the red snow fence.

No one moved off the bench until Leaping Frog rounded second. Then, at last, the players seemed to realize that the Indian shortstop had just won the ball game for the Ludell Leapers, 3-2. Leaping Frog was just stepping on the blue third base and heading toward home when the heavens opened.

A giant funnel swooped down from the black clouds. It kicked dust and debris one hundred yards into the air behind center field. It moved swiftly toward the softball diamond. A telephone pole in its path cracked like a toothpick.

Clyde saw the twisting prairie monster first and grabbed Rand by the arm, yelling, "Run for the schoolhouse basement. It's a tornado!" He motioned to the Atwood bench and the spectators to follow, and they all raced toward the Ludell school building nearby.

There was no order during the rush toward the brick building precious seconds away. Fear of death by a wild wind became an individual nightmare. Frantic footsteps crunched over the buffalo grass, past the outfield fence, and into the school yard. Clyde was the first to reach the locked back door. He quickly removed his shoe and broke the glass, reached in, and unlocked the door.

In the excitement, the players had bunched so closely behind Clyde that he couldn't get his arm back to open the door. Leaping Frog sensed the problem and let fly with a quick forearm blow, decking the front three teammates and Rand.

There was no order during the rush . . .

While Rand and the other unfortunates were scrambling to their feet, Clyde, Leaping Frog and the rest raced down the stone steps into the Ludell school basement. Rand was the last to climb from the bottom of the pile and quickly glanced over his shoulder at the sky. A howling funnel hovering near second base started swiftly toward the schoolhouse.

Rand leaped for the open basement door. In his excitement, he jumped too far and fell, rolling and tumbling, down the steps to the bottom. He landed in a world of darkness. Rusty hinges surrendered to the enraged wind, hurling the door into the violent world. Debris fell into the basement and ears popped as the wind slammed the brick structure. Rand tried to clear his head. His hands rubbed over the floor as he felt his surroundings in the darkness.

"That you, Rand?" yelled Clyde. Rand reached out and grabbed Clyde's leg. "Yeah. Man alive! That's some wind out there!"

"You okay?"

"Yeah," said Rand. "Bumped my head a little falling down the stairs, but I'm okay now. Is everybody in here? Leaping Frog?"

Everyone started talking and shouting at each other. "I'm here," came Leaping Frog's voice out of the darkness. "Just about six feet away."

"Where's everybody else?" asked Rand.

"We're here," yelled Dirty Mutt from the other end of the cellar. "Everybody from Atwood's okay. Nobody's hurt. You guys all right?"

Clyde shouted back that the Ludell players and parents were okay and that they would all sit tight until the storm passed. Silence enveloped the cellar as the twister raged.

Rand's thoughts drifted back to the New York Mets and hurler Tom Seaver, miles away, probably playing in the comfort of Shea Stadium right then. He wondered if a Met player had ever had to slide down a flight of stairs in his climb to make the Big League. He couldn't picture a Met player —any Big League player for that matter—racing away from Shea Stadium, across a buffalo grass outfield, and into a basement cellar in a headlong slide. His mind whirled, with player after player sliding into the basement near the stadium. But each time, the player slid instead into the dirt of the Ludell school cellar.

Rand's thoughts were miles away from the cellar and a sinking feeling was now winding to the pit of his stomach. He felt like a lonely coyote miles away from anyone and everything, lost in a world of blackness. Suddenly, Leaping Frog grabbed his leg and brought him back to the present. "Hey, Rand. You okay? You haven't said a word for awhile."

Rand cleared his throat. "I'm all right. Just thinking."

"I remember my first tornado," said Leaping Frog. "We were on the reservation and visiting my grandfather, Running Bear. The wind was howling like it is now and I must have been about eight years old." Rand could hear him shift his position in the darkness. "Boy, I was scared. We made a mad dash for a dugout and waited for the storm to die out."

"Did it blow over your house?" asked Rand.

"Naw. Didn't do much damage. Just touched down once. Ripped out a couple of trees, but that's about all. I was still scared."

The noise of the wind rushing past the school building outside interrupted the conversation, but Leaping Frog went on more loudly, "Still remember what my grandfather said to me that day. Sure knew how to make a scared one feel better."

"I'd like to know," said Rand quickly. He paused, "I mean, I've always wondered what old Indians said about tornadoes."

"Well. He'd tell us the same thing every time the wind blew and I bet he told me the story a thousand times. He'd say, 'The wind is a friend, but it brings snow and ice slanting across the plains and bends the trees and make them angry. The wind holds the vulture motionless in the sky, tears at the lodge coverings, whispers in the prairie grass, and screams like a crazy woman. The wind sends the fire across the prairie, causing the children to flee and sends the crazy dancer, the tornado, down from the clouds to chase them to the sumac and oak saplings and to cling tightly to the trees that bend to the fury of the wind. The wind aids the hunter, brings to him the scent of the buffalo. It brings secret messages to the camp dogs. It hides the noise of the hunter's approach, as well as that of the warriors. The wind brings the odor of the campfire to the hunter. It lifts the dust of the travois high into the air like smoke.' "

Leaping Frog paused. He had ripped off the words of his grandfather without stumbling, all from memory, and the Indian folklore seemed to spur him even further.

"You know," said Leaping Frog, "even in those days, my people knew what to do when it stormed. My grandfather would say they would watch the tail of a tornado swing like a rope to the earth, hissing loudly like a snake, and then they would run to the cane stems, the running oaks, or the sumac, to lie flat on their stomachs and hug tightly to Mother Earth. If hail came, the warriors would hold buffalo hides over their heads. If the lightning came, the young warriors would sing. It was said that a warrior's song could turn the wind into a prairie breeze and challenge the lightning and the death songs over the land."

"Say," said Rand. "Maybe we ought to sing!"

"Good idea," echoed Clyde's voice in the darkness. "Let's sing 'Home on the Range.' "

Clyde belted out the first words of the early pioneer song and the others slowly joined in. Rand didn't know it all, but he stumbled through the first stanza, repeating the words after Clyde.

Outside, the wind beat itself against the rural schoolhouse, while underneath, in a dirt-covered storm cellar, a group of softball players, their parents, and a proud young Indian sat singing in the darkness.

Chapter 8

The storm's fury soon passed. Anxious parents began arriving at the deserted ball park. The players had crawled from their dark haven and were standing beside the schoolhouse when Clyde's parents arrived.

"Are you boys okay?" asked Clyde's father.

"Yeah. But lucky for the storm cellar or we might have been blown away! Did you see that big tornado from the farm?" asked Clyde.

"Sure did. We were so worried about you when we saw the storm come up that quickly," said Clyde's mother. "It apparently only hit here."

The trio climbed into the back seat. Clyde's father turned the car around to survey the damage. Luckily, the tornado had only touched down in several places in its mad dash for earthly power.

The first base bag was behind center field, where a large cottonwood had been uprooted. The wild wind had completely lifted the tree out of the ground. It was as if an insane giant had pulled the forty-foot tree out by the roots and then slammed it down to the earth to die. In the brightness of the car lights, they could see that a six-foot hole gaped where the tree had been. From there, the tornado had raced straight for the school, missing most of the playing field.

The cellar door of the school had been hurled thirty feet away and was wedged in the branches of another cottonwood. The school building itself had suffered only minor damage as the rigid brick structure had withstood the wind.

Clyde's father turned the car and headed back toward the main entrance where the pickup was still parked. Rand suddenly grabbed his shoulder. "Stop, Uncle Roger! There's home plate."

The car lights flashed on the broken form of home plate lying near the entrance to the ball park. Rand turned toward Leaping Frog. "Did you touch home plate?"

"Did I WHAT?"

"Come on! Did you step on home plate?"

"I don't remember," said Leaping Frog. "It doesn't matter now."

78

"It *does* matter now," replied Rand, reaching to open the door. "Come on. Go touch home plate. We want to make sure we win fair and square. Otherwise, it's still a tie ball game."

Clyde looked at Leaping Frog and shrugged his shoulders. The Indian reluctantly got out of the car and ambled over to touch the remains of home plate. He hurried back as if he didn't want anyone to see him.

"You satisfied, hot shot?"

"Almost," replied Rand. "We've still got to get the equipment. While you were touching home, I saw most of it over by the fence."

The boys scurried out of the car and gathered up the bats and balls and pieces of softball gear. They climbed back into the car and dumped it all on the floor. They would come back to get the pickup tomorrow. They were tired. It had been a hectic night.

Chapter 9

The wild summer storm failed to dampen Rand's enthusiasm for his new love of slow-pitch softball, nor did it slow the team's winning ways. The Leapers played seven more games over the next four weeks, winning all by a lopsided score, including a rematch with Atwood.

The team had put it all together and was playing well as a unit. Leaping Frog's fielding had been the cement that had pulled the team together. He was the friend, the sparkplug, and the fielder. Whenever something was lacking in a game, Leaping Frog always came up with what was needed. He still refused to use a glove, but his fielding did not suffer. His performance inspired the other players to do their jobs well.

Rand had called for two practices before the state tournament, only three nights away. He wanted to make sure he would be able to go home to New York at the end of the summer and tell his friends he had played and co-managed a state championship team.

He wanted, also, to make sure the team didn't go flat. Game after game, the team had performed well enough to win, but the state tournament would mean more pressure. A loss would signal the end, and by a strange tournament rule, Ludell had to win two games the first night to advance to the finals. Six teams had been selected for the tournament with two teams awarded byes.

The Ludell Leapers had drawn Oscage City in the first game of the tournament, and the winner would play Colby in the second game of the doubleheader. The other teams would play the next night and the winners would then play for the junior division state championship.

The Leapers had played every game without uniforms and Rand, being a true-blue baseball fan, refused to change now. Dirty Mutt suggested they all wear the same color shirts, but Rand's baseball superstitions wouldn't allow that. He and Clyde ordered the players to wear whatever they liked for the opening game. Neither one wanted to break with tradition now that the season boiled down to a win or lose situation.

Rand and Clyde had programmed the pre-tournament practice sessions down to how many ground balls would be hit to each infielder. The first practice would be devoted entirely to hitting and the next session to fielding. Rand insisted the squad hold a meeting before fielding practice to discuss slow-pitch rules. He wanted to make sure the games were won or lost on the merits of both teams, and not by mental mistakes.

The first two sessions went smoothly. The co-managers were pleased with both the hitting and fielding. Matt and Patt were especially outstanding in the outfield.

Clyde's fielding also improved. Because of his size, he had a tendency to rush the ball off balance and try to field it while stumbling forward. At practice, Rand suggested Clyde hesitate more before rushing full speed toward the ball. That tactic seemed to work better. Clyde had an arm like a toy cannon, and the split-second hesitation seemed to boost his confidence. He booted only one of fifteen ground balls and made some outstanding plays.

Rand thought he looked more like a second baseman of the New York Mets than a sawed-off softball player. He only missed one ground ball during the practice and that was because of a bad hop.

Leaping Frog refused to be outdone. When his turn came he handled chance after chance flawlessly. On the last ground ball, he roamed far to his left near second base, only to have the ball jump, spinning off a dirt clod, high in the air at the last moment. He slid past the ball, but with catlike reflexes somehow managed to knock it down. He grabbed the ball and, from his knees, threw it to Tommy in one motion.

Tommy finished infield practice. The first sacker was actually the weakest fielder on the team, but few balls were ever hit to him because of Willie's pinpoint pitching. With Rand's range at second, he could concentrate on taking the throws.

"Remember," yelled Rand as the players finished running laps to close out practice. "Wear what you like . . . jeans . . . sweat shirts . . . cutoffs. We'll all meet here tomorrow at two o'clock. Clyde's and Tommy's dads are taking cars. Our game starts at six, and if we win, we'll play again at nine. Be ready, guys. Be ready."

He patted Clyde on the seat and trotted to the pickup. Tomorrow would be the high point or downfall of the season. No more innovations, no more new theories to be tested. The team would now have to prove itself on the field. Tomorrow, for Rand, at least, seemed too far away.

Chapter 10

The sun was high in the sky as Clyde and Rand climbed into the car with Uncle Roger. It had been a long night and morning for the pair. Clyde had slept fairly well, but Rand had tossed and turned all night. He couldn't pinpoint the trouble, but had an uneasy feeling in the pit of his stomach. And to top it all off, the telephone call from Leaping Frog hadn't eased the situation. What the Indian had asked didn't seem to be a problem in itself, but there was something in the tone of his voice that was strange. First he said his uncle would drive him in, and then he asked if he could really wear something besides his jeans and a sweat shirt. Rand had told him again to wear what he wanted.

Butterflies were turning somersaults in Rand's

stomach as they headed toward the playing field to meet the rest of the team.

When they arrived, most of the players were already waiting. Rand looked past Willie, Patt, Matt, Tommy, and Dirty Mutt. Everyone was there but Leaping Frog.

Rand looked at his watch. They were scheduled to leave in five minutes. He shook his head. "It's not like Leaping Frog to be late."

"Relax," replied Clyde, patting him on the shoulder. "Everything's going to be all right. He'll be here in a minute, ready for action."

Clyde had barely gotten the word "action" out of his mouth when a black pickup rounded the corner in front of the softball diamond. It belonged to Leaping Frog's uncle.

Rand heaved a sigh of relief and turned his attention to his managing chores. He wanted to make sure all of the equipment was accounted for, and the car ride situation was worked out correctly. His back was turned and he was studying his lists of cars, players, and equipment when he heard the pickup stop and the door slam. He was trying to decide if he should ride with Clyde when someone tugged at his shirt.

"Rand, Rand!" Clyde whispered.

"Talk to you in a second," replied Rand. "Got

"You've changed. You . . . you . . ."

to be sure that everyone has a ride."

"You had better look around," said Clyde, pulling roughly at Rand's shirt. "We've got a problem. A REAL problem!"

Rand turned quickly to see his shortstop standing nearby, grinning like a Cheshire cat and clad in Indian deerskins. The grin widened at Rand's horrified stare. The co-manager's mouth almost dropped to the playing field at what he saw.

"You've changed. You . . . you . . ." He couldn't spit the words out. He shook his head to try, but Leaping Frog finished his sentence.

"You're a girl!" she said. "That's right," and she walked closer to Rand and Clyde. "I thought you had guessed about me being a girl by now."

Rand looked at Clyde, who had a silly expression on his face. Dropping his clipboard to the ground and smashing his toe, Rand turned back to stare closely at his shortstop. A midcalf-length deerskin dress draped over the Indian maiden, subtly changing the heavy muscles by the way it clung. Brightly colored beads decorated it, and there was a leather fringe on each sleeve. Additional strands of leather danced above buckskin moccasins.

"But . . . but . . ." The words still didn't seem to come very well. "I mean . . . well . . .

87

what kind of a name is that for a real live girl?"

"What do you mean?" demanded Leaping Frog, and her hands shot out toward Rand's shirt collar.

Rand backed up. "Well, you know. Girls have names like Janie, Margaret, Mary, Nellie, Letha, and stuff like that."

"My people don't," replied Leaping Frog. "And I figure Leaping is as good a name for a woman as any."

Rand didn't reply, nor did Clyde, Dirty Mutt, Tommy, or the rest of the players. They were all as shocked as the cousins.

Leaping Frog tried to explain. "I didn't tell you guys at first I was a girl because I was afraid you'd kick me off the team."

She stepped directly in front of Rand. "After talking about Indians and women that night, it convinced me I had to be what I am. And that time in the cellar—I was proud to be an Indian. So I started thinking, I've got to be proud to be a woman, too. I'm an Indian and a woman and it's time everyone knows about it."

Rand wanted to ask her why she had to pick tonight to be proud to be a woman but he didn't say anything.

Finally, Clyde nudged his co-manager. "Er . . . ah . . . what are we going to do?"

"What do you mean," interrupted Leaping Frog, "saying 'What are we going to do?' Are we playing for the state championship tonight or not?"

There was silence again and Rand was trying to sort out his thoughts. "We were. But with a girl and all I just don't see . . ."

"Don't see what?" interrupted Leaping Frog, her temper rising like a flash flood. "Are you saying there's something different about me now since you've found out I'm a girl?"

"No," replied Rand. "I'm just saying I don't know if . . . well . . . if we want to play . . . that's all."

" 'Don't know if you want to play!' " repeated Leaping Frog. "That's all you've been harping about ever since you got here. Got to win every game or die. You came and got me to play in the first place, remember? Well, just because I'm a girl doesn't mean I can't play now." Her voice was suddenly soft. "Does it?"

Rand didn't answer.

"Well. Does it?"

"We WANT you to play," said Rand, rather hesitantly. "It's just I don't know about the rules . . . and all." He turned to Clyde

"Don't look at me," echoed Clyde.

"Now come on," pleaded Rand, pushing at his cousin. "You know softball rules better than I do. Can girls play in the state tournament or not?"

"Why not?" asked Clyde. "If she's good enough. And we know Leaping Frog is as good as anybody."

Rand was still in a dilemma. He hadn't expected his star shortstop to turn out to be a girl in the first place. Nor had he expected her to come to play in the most important game of the season in a dress.

He kicked at the grass. "I guess you can play. Haven't seen any rules against females. I know you are the right age." He paused. "But what about that ridiculous skirt?"

"RAND," burst out Leaping Frog. Her mouth turned downward. "You SAID to wear whatever I wanted to." She seemed crushed. Her eyes cast down to the buffalo grass in front of her. "My uncle wanted me to wear it." She paused and toed a small clump of grass. "It . . . it was my aunt's tribal dress before she died last summer. He thought it might bring good luck to the team."

There was silence for several moments as Leaping Frog stood looking at the grass. She suddenly bolted toward uncle Uncle Roger's car, threw open the door, and fell crying into the back seat.

Rand could feel the chill of the others. He hadn't expected Leaping Frog to be so sensitive. Playing shortstop in a long skirt seemed awfully silly to him and might hurt the team's chance at victory. It could be hard to win a state tournament with a shortstop dressed like Sacajawea.

His mind clouded with pictures of Leaping Frog in a sweat shirt sliding across home plate, ranging far behind second to make a play. Then he saw Clyde holding a trophy high over his head and the players carrying Rand on their shoulders. But that all faded to a picture of Leaping Frog standing in front of the team in a long fringed dress.

Rand wanted to hide, but it was time to make a decision.

He walked toward the car. "Let's go," said Rand. "If we don't hurry we'll never make the game on time." The others followed. The state tourney was only hours away.

Chapter 11

It was a half hour before game time when the Ludell Leapers arrived at the site of the slow-pitch state tournament in Barnard.

The town was nestled in the center of a long valley. Wide flood-control dikes, looking like the Great Wall of China, circled the town of some two hundred people.

The sleepy little village was full of vacant buildings. A theater with a giant CLOSED sign across its main window seemed accurately to portray the economy of the town. A small billfold-size picture of a young John Wayne yellowed in the far corner of the window.

But, despite its outward appearance and its look of economic bust, the little town of Barnard was a hotbed for the softball tournament.

A crowd had gathered and a muffled roar of excitement was in the air. A parking area had been reserved for the players behind a brightly painted grandstand. It was a wooden structure built in the days of the depression in the 1930's, and the Kansas decades hadn't been too kind. The warped wooden seats were already more than half-filled with fans. Outside restrooms, called "outhouses," sat majestically on each side of the stadium. A fresh coat of paint vainly tried to disguise their age.

The playing field was surrounded by cars in which people were sitting either to avoid the mosquitoes or to watch the many small children who were running around. A group of boys were having a quick game of stick ball by the lone cottonwood tree in right field.

Rand could feel the butterflies that had been resting in his stomach start the climb to his throat. His heart was pounding wildly. He led the team through a chicken-wire gate into the stadium. He looked toward first base where the Oscage City Ravens were warming up.

Wild laughter belched out from one huddle of players as they spotted Leaping Frog. The Ludell Leapers started tossing several balls back and forth. Rand was placing the bats in a rack when he suddenly felt a firm hand on his shoulder.

"Hey, buddy. You the manager?"

Rand nodded. "I'm a co-manager."

"Well," said a heavy-set man with arms that looked as if they belonged on a blacksmith a century before. "You ain't allowed to bring your girl friend in. This is only for players. Sorry, little fella."

"She's a player," replied Rand.

The muscle man popped his eyes. "Well! Don't know. Never had a girl in the tournament before. It really ain't like a girl." He stood for several more seconds nodding his head and talking to himself. "No, sir. Just never had a girl, fella, good enough to play in a state tournament before."

Rand went back to putting the bats in the rack. The man shook his head and walked out of the chicken-wire gate and climbed the wooden steps of the grandstand to a bald-headed man who was sitting behind a small table at the loud-speaker. They exchanged whispers, and the bald-headed man grinned at the muscle man and followed him down a flight of stairs to the other side of the playing field. They motioned to the manager of the Oscage City Ravens.

Rand finished sorting the equipment and joined in tossing a ball back and forth with Clyde. He spotted the muscle man waving from across the diamond. Rand threw his glove aside and trotted over to the corner of the field where the men were standing.

"This here is the tournament director," said the muscle man, putting a huge arm around the bald-headed man. "And this here is the Oscage City manager."

"We've never had a girl in a game before," said the tournament director. "Especially a girl wearing a long Indian dress." He grinned at the muscle man and the Oscage City manager, and looked sternly at Rand. "We don't actually have a rule that says you can't have a girl on your team." He paused and looked down at the papers in his hands. "And we don't actually have any rule that says you've got to wear uniforms." He paused again.

"Well. What's the problem?" asked Rand.

"Hey, Sam," interrupted the muscle man. "They ain't got but eight players all told." He nudged the director. "You said these guys haven't lost a game?" He shook his head. "Seems kind of funny. A team playing with a girl and only having eight players. Sure seems funny."

The director put his hand on Rand's shoulder. "We don't have any rules against your team. But

"What's the problem?" asked Rand.

you do have an unusual team. No uniforms, only eight players, and a girl in a long dress, and, you see, this is a state tournament.

Rand nodded. "I know. You got anything else to say?" He held his breath.

The director merely shook his head. The Oscage City manager grinned at the boy. "Hope your gal friend is ready to play."

"We're ready," replied Rand. He started to walk away and then stopped short. "Hope YOU'RE ready."

The manager laughed out loud. He took off his baseball cap and slapped it against his leg. "We're ready, boy. We're ready. Don't you worry."

Chapter 12

The grandstand was completely filled with fans, and cars encircled the ball park. The Ludell Leapers had been designated as the home team and had taken the field. Willie ambled to the mound and lobbed several pitches toward the plate.

The fans buzzed as Leaping Frog, her dress fringes flying in the wind, trotted to her position at shortstop. She looked rather out of place in a white man's game, dressed in the costume of her ancestors. Tommy threw a slow roller to Leaping Frog, who fielded the ball cleanly and flicked it back perfectly to the first sacker.

The Oscage City manager was sitting on the far end of the player's bench. After watching Leaping Frog field another infield grounder from the first baseman and return it quickly, he walked over to the plate umpire and murmured something in his ear.

The plate umpire motioned toward Rand, and yelled, "Your shortstop don't have a glove."

"Don't need the glove," interrupted Leaping Frog. "My hands have been working pretty well without one. Wasn't born with a glove."

The umpire shrugged his shoulders, pulled the face mask on his head, and walked behind the plate. He barked out, "Play ball!"

The fans roared, and the manager slapped the side of his leg with his cap. He tapped the first hitter on the seat of his pants and trotted over to the bench.

The hitter stepped in. He was a small, right-handed batter, who pushed his feet firmly into the freshly dragged dirt. He looked intently toward Willie, who was gripping and regripping the large softball behind his back. Willie flipped an extra high spinning inside pitch. The Oscage City batter swung hard, but only topped the ball weakly toward Clyde at third. The third sacker took several steps, fielded the ball cleanly, and rifled a perfect strike to Tommy at first base, beating the runner by six steps.

The next hitter took a chest-high strike and lashed out at an inside floating knuckleball. The

99

ball headed toward the hole between Clyde and Leaping Frog. The Indian took two giant steps, reached down with her bare right hand, picked the ball cleanly from the dirt, and fired a chest-high bullet to first base before falling in a heap beside Clyde.

Rand looked at the Raven manager, whose mouth seemed to have dropped wide open. The man took his hat off and rubbed his head as if he couldn't believe what he had just seen.

The fans seemed almost as stunned at the ease with which the Indian girl had thrown out the runner. Then, as if on cue, a scattering of applause rippled through the grandstand.

Fans in their cars refused to be outdone. They suddenly beat on their horns in approval of the outstanding play.

The crowd was still buzzing when the next hitter stepped in. He swung at the first pitch and lofted a high fly to Patt in right field for the third out. A few cars were still honking as the Ludell Leapers moved in to bat in the last half of the first inning. The Oscage City boosters booed, uncertain of what was to follow.

Matt led off for the Leapers. He let two pitches go by and then slapped the ball past the first base bag and raced around that base and slid headlong into second with the game's first hit. Rand was the next hitter and he promptly jumped on the first pitch and stroked it down the third base line for a single. Matt raced home with the first score of the game.

Rand hadn't been impressed with the pitching of the Oscage City hurler, and he gleefully waited for the power hitters to come up. Clyde gripped the bat tightly as he strolled toward the plate. The pitcher took a quick windup and sent a soft, floating spinner toward the plate. Clyde's eyes flashed as he waited for it to come down. He uncoiled as the ball neared the strike zone. The sound of the bat crushing into the ball was like a flyswatter hitting a flat table. The ball climbed quickly into the dry Kansas air and cleared the right-field fence. A pack of young boys chased after it as it rolled along the prairie.

The crowd roared and the cars honked at the excitement the Ludell Leapers were creating in the very first inning. The crowd was still buzzing when Leaping Frog stepped into the batter's box. The Oscage City manager was pacing nervously in front of the bench, yelling encouragement to his team. "Come on, you guys," he barked. "Let's get tough. Got an easy one here. An Indian squaw. She'll swing like an old woman. Make her eat dirt, like the cavalry did to her ancestors. Give her a taste of sodbuster dirt."

Leaping Frog moved uneasily, but settled down quickly as the pitcher started his delivery. As the first pitch started down in its arch toward the plate, Leaping Frog uncoiled, swinging hard. The bat sailed out of her hands and rolled swiftly toward the Oscage City manager. He jumped to avoid it and landed in a heap. The bat sailed on past, slamming into the fence behind.

"Sorry," yelled Leaping Frog. "The bat must have slipped." She said each word as if she had acid on her tongue. "Us Indian squaws can't hangum on to white man's bats. Need sodbuster dirt on hands. Makeum hands work better." She reached down and grabbed a handful of dirt and walked over to pick up the bat.

The startled manager sat on the ground with his cap half-cocked on his head and a puzzled look across his face. When the pitcher released the next pitch, he struggled to his feet as Leaping Frog lashed out.

The ball was cracked on a straight line five feet off the ground directly over the manager. He quickly threw himself face down to avoid it. He stood up and dusted himself off, and walked briskly to the far corner of the player's bench. He sat staring blankly into space and blinking wildly at the sudden turn of events. The crowd roared at his predicament. One bald, big-bellied fan in the front row of the grandstand belched out a wild laugh and beat his feet on the ground.

Leaping Frog stepped back in the batter's box. She lined the next pitch down the third base line for a double, and scored seconds later when Patt drilled a single past the first sacker.

The rest of the inning was filled with base hits and scores for the Ludell Leapers, even with two changes of pitchers. Base hits fell from one corner of the field to the other, and before the inning was over, the Ludell Leapers had scored eleven runs. Clyde had hit a home run and a double, Rand a single and a double, and Leaping Frog a single and a double.

After the wild exchange with Leaping Frog, the manager remained quietly on the far corner of the bench, watching sadly as his team was slaughtered. The game was called when Leaping Frog stepped on home plate with the twenty-first run. Under a tournament rule, games were called when one team led by twenty-one runs.

Colby promptly took the field to warm up for the next game. The Ludell Leapers had advanced one step closer to the state championship! They would play Colby in a half hour. But for now, they would relax and prepare mentally for the second step in the battle to win the championship.

Chapter 13

The sun was slipping behind the horizon, and the grandstand was casting shadows over much of the playing field when the Ludell Leapers walked back into the Barnard stadium to play the Colby Eagles.

Rand and Clyde had been impressed, watching Colby warm up. Their pitcher, a tall left-hander, had a natural curve and a double-pump windup. The motion was deceptive and Colby seemed able to play good defense behind him. And unlike Willie, who had only seven players to back him up, the Colby hurler had nine.

Rand had faith in the defensive play of the Leapers, and he knew Willie would be hard to hit. Unlike baseball pitchers, softball hurlers could pitch every day for a month, if necessary, without hurting their arms. Willie was warming up on the sidelines for the second game.

Ludell took infield practice first and then watched the Colby Eagles go through a dazzling display of fielding without committing an error. The Colby left-hander walked to the mound to begin the last game of the evening.

The umpire motioned to the Ludell bench for the first hitter to step into the box. Patt pushed his feet down into the loose dirt and waved his bat menacingly at the tall left-hander. He watched a roundhouse curve float by for a strike and then topped a grounder to the shortstop. The Colby infielder moved in quickly and fired a perfect strike to the first baseman for an out. Rand stepped in next and hit a looping first pitch toward short center field. The fourth outfielder raced to his left and made a shoestring catch for the second out. Clyde then jumped on the first pitch and lined out deep to the right fielder. In four pitches, the Ludell Leapers had gone down in order for the first time in the tournament. Clyde patted his cousin on the back and they trotted out to their positions.

Out of the corner of his eye, Rand could see the Colby manager on the sidelines talking to his players. He was whispering to the lead-off hitter, a short, blond second baseman. Rand fielded a practice slow roller from the first sacker, flipping it underhanded from the pocket of his glove back to Tommy.

The Colby lead-off hitter stepped in. Rand watched him closely as he choked up three inches on the bat, placed his front foot inches from the plate, and pointed it toward left field. On the first pitch, Willie curled a high lob to the inside of the plate. The Colby hitter leaned away from the ball and stroked a hit past Rand and Tommy. Matt raced to his left and quickly fired the ball to the infield to keep the first hit of the game to a single.

The next hitter, a long-legged center fielder, stepped into the box and also positioned his feet toward the left-field line. He poked the first pitch in the same spot for a single. The lead-off hitter raced into third and the Colby Eagles had the first scoring threat of the evening. The Colby shortstop moved in and again on the first pitch stroked at the ball. The ball rolled past Rand and the first runner scored and another raced to third. The Colby Eagles looked as if they were going to break the game wide open. Rand motioned for Clyde to join him at the mound, and signaled to the umpire for a time-out.

"Got a plan," said Rand taking the ball from Willie, who looked dejectedly at his feet.

"Shoot," said Clyde. "We'd better do something quick."

"Well. I want you to play on my side of second base with me."

"You want me to WHAT?"

"I want you to play on my side of second base. That way they can't push the ball past the right side of the infield." Rand grabbed Clyde by the arm. "Their manager is having them hit it to the right side. And I don't think they will hit the ball well to the left side, because Willie will keep mixing the ball up. And we've got Leaping Frog to cover there. She fields like a vacuum cleaner. She'll be able to take care of anything hit that way."

Clyde shook his head. "I guess, Rand, you know this game is the big one. It's win or else it's all over."

Rand nodded. "No one's hit Willie good all year and those Colby guys have just been pushing the ball. They won't get much wood on it. I'm betting the plan will work."

"Like betting a state championship?" asked Clyde.

Rand nodded. "Yeah. I guess like betting a state championship."

Clyde trotted over and told Leaping Frog of the

game plan and joined Rand on the first base side of second. Rand motioned for the outfielders to play their normal positions.

After Willie stepped back on the mound and the fans realized the odd defensive set-up was for real, a ripple of noise waved through the crowd. The umpire stepped from behind the plate and pointed toward Rand.

"Hey, fella. You ready or are you playing some kind of trick on me?"

"We're ready," barked Rand. "We're ready."

The next hitter stepped into the batter's box and took the first pitch for a strike. On the next pitch, he knocked it directly toward Rand's new position. The New York second baseman didn't have time to get the runner scoring but threw to first for the first out of the inning. Several cars honked and scattered applause echoed from the grandstand.

The Colby manager walked over to his next hitter, said something, and ran back toward the players' bench. The hitter took the first pitch from Willie and then swung hard at an outside pitch. It was a roller toward Leaping Frog, playing half-way between second and third. She scooped it up in her bare hands and threw out the runner for the second out. Rand could feel a new surge of excitement come back into the players and he found himself winking at Leaping Frog.

The next hitter swung at the first pitch and lofted it high over the pitcher's mound. Rand called for it, took it for the third out, and the first inning was history. Colby had the lead, 2-0.

The Leapers continued to have trouble hitting the Colby hurler in the next innings but scored a run in the fourth when Clyde and Leaping Frog slammed back-to-back doubles. Rand's unusual defensive set-up was working and Willie was doing his part as well. He kept the hitters off stride with his pinpoint control. Leaping Frog made several outstanding defensive plays, including one in which she roamed over to third to spear a high hopper.

The score remained 2-1 through the fifth, as Rand grabbed two bats to open the top of the sixth. He had popped up the first time when he was fooled on an inside curve, and had grounded out weakly to third when he tried to pull an outside pitch. This time, he told himself, he was going to hit the ball where it was pitched, go for a single so the power hitters could bring him home. He knew he had to pick out his pitch. Otherwise, it would be his last time at bat in the state tournament.

Rand stepped in and eyed the left-hander closely. He watched the first pitch sail past on the outside corner of the plate for a strike. He took a deep breath, clenched his hands, and raised the bat high off his shoulder. The Colby pitcher took a double windup and flipped an extra high lob toward Rand.

He waited patiently for the ball to come down. As it entered the strike zone on the inside of the plate, he whipped the bat around, sending a vicious line drive past the third baseman into the left-field corner. He took a wide turn at first and threw his body headfirst into second. The crowd roared and the Ludell fans went wild. They were trailing by one, and Clyde was at the plate, followed by Leaping Frog, and the chances for a state championship were not over.

Clyde stomped the ground and frowned toward the pitcher. He swung wickedly at the first pitch, missing the ball by inches, then took the next pitch. On the very next pitch, he poked it past the second baseman for a single. Rand rounded third and started for home, but, out of the corner of his eye, he could see the outfielder getting set to throw to the plate. He stopped and raced back to third base. The throw to the plate was perfect and Rand would have been out by ten feet. On the throw,

. . . threw his body headfirst into second

Clyde raced into second. Rand could feel his heart pounding as if it had been resting all day, just waiting for this moment.

Leaping Frog grabbed a handful of dirt, rubbed it off on her deerskins, and waved the bat high above her head. The Colby pitcher looked toward the plate, took one pump, then a second warm-up, then a third, and lobbed the ball extra high. The Indian girl waited and then swung with all her might. The ball seemed to jump off the bat, and it sounded as if it had been hit by a Ping-Pong paddle. It arched high over the third baseman, over the left fielder, and over the outfield fence.

The fans in the cars went wild, honking as if they hadn't ever used a car horn before. Rand touched home plate, and, seconds later, so did Clyde. The Ludell bench had emptied and the Leapers were standing around home plate, pounding each other, waiting for Leaping Frog to round third and come home. A giant smile flashed across her face as she stepped on third. She slowed a split second before stepping on home and then hit the plate with both feet and threw herself at her teammates.

Rand was at the front of the welcoming committee and was immediately knocked to the ground in the excitement. Clyde picked Leaping Frog up by the waist and the two were pounded on all sides by their teammates. Rand was still rolled in a ball beneath the players' feet when he felt a sharp poke on the shoulder.

"Say, little fella. You asleep or something?" The umpire grinned slyly.

Rand didn't answer but slowly rose to his feet and followed the Leapers to the bench.

The umpire dusted off home plate and called for play to resume. It was almost academic, but Patt picked up another hit before Colby got the Leapers out in order in the sixth.

Willie was superb in the bottom of the sixth and retired the Eagles in order. However, the Leapers failed to score any more runs in the top of the seventh and took to the field to try and preserve their two-run lead in the last inning.

It seemed that Willie's double joints had stretched in the excitement and he was hiding the ball twice as long behind his back, flipping it out at the last moment to further confuse Colby.

The first Colby hitter lifted a lazy pop-up to Rand at second, and, on the very next pitch, the Colby left fielder hit a slow roller to Clyde, who was still playing near second, for the second out of the inning. Willie took a long breath, stepped off the mound, and then stepped back on the rubber.

He flipped an extra high lob on the next pitch to the tall, muscular clean-up hitter. The Colby ace waited patiently and then lashed hard at the pitch. He hit down on the ball, but still managed to get good wood on it. The ball rolled quickly toward Leaping Frog's left, but she was ready. She took two long steps, grabbed the ball with both hands, and uncoiled, whipping a perfect strike to Tommy for the last out of the game.

The players all rushed to Willie on the mound, pounding each other wildly. Rand was standing alone behind the excitement to watch the Colby manager. Totally frustrated by the defeat, the older man stormed from the bench and grabbed the umpire. But for now, Rand could care less. He and the Ludell Leapers were happy. They had once more produced on the field, and were now only one game away from the state championship.

Chapter 14

On the day of the state championship, Rand was feeling good. He had received a call from his parents to wish him good luck in the game. He was feeling so happy that he had called Leaping Frog and asked her to be sure to wear the deer-skins again. He told her she had looked nice in them, but the real truth was that he was supersti-tious. They had just won the biggest games of the year with her in a tribal costume and he wasn't about to throw away a good luck omen.

The team arrived at the Barnard stadium an hour before game time. The stands were already filling when the Leapers walked in through the chicken-wire gate and started warming up.

Rand threw the bag of bats near the bat rack. This was *the* game. The state championship. The very thing he had thought about on the steps of his New York home. This was the chance to play for glory. This was the time to prove who was the best.

The Ludell Leapers were meeting the Garden City Buffaloes, winners of the other bracket of the tournament. The Buffaloes were on the first base side of the field, tossing balls back and forth, dressed in Kelly green uniforms and pale yellow socks. Garden City was undefeated and probably the sharpest-looking team in the tournament. A twelve-piece pep band at the far corner of the stadium was belting out John Philip Sousa marches.

The Leapers took a short infield practice and watched Garden City take to the field. In their dazzling uniforms, the Buffaloes were impressive. They chattered like a flock of birds and whipped the ball around the infield with a lot of zip. The pitcher, a roly-poly, dark-skinned youth, finished his warm-up pitches on the sidelines and walked to the mound. He took four quick warm-up pitches there and stood straight for the National Anthem.

Rand's mind was miles from the "bombs bursting in air." His head was full of a giant trophy, and the Leapers carrying him off the field in victory. But even his mind full of glory couldn't convince the butterflies in his stomach to slow down

116

to at least a leisurely flight. The applause and shouts from his teammates brought him back to the game.

Patt led off, took the first pitch for a strike, and then lashed a single past the third baseman. Rand strolled to the plate and place-hit a single past the third baseman. Patt raced to third. Clyde followed with a towering blast to right field. The right fielder played him perfectly for an out, but Patt scored on the sacrifice fly.

Leaping Frog then stepped in. She waved the bat high above her head. She watched two pitches go by and then hit a screaming line drive into the left-field corner. Rand raced around the bases to score standing up, and Leaping Frog stormed into third with a triple. The game was just minutes old, and the Ludell Leapers had pulled into a 2-0 lead. They scored another run seconds later on an infield out and trotted to the field in the first inning in the state championship game with a three-run lead.

The Garden City lead-off hitter showed his team wasn't going to fold as he lashed at the first pitch for a single. The second hitter followed with a slow roller to Rand at second. It was too late for the runner at second, but he threw the hitter out. The next man dropped a fly ball in front of Patt in the outfield and the runner scored to cut the lead to 3-1. Leaping Frog threw out the next hitter on a sparkling play from deep in the hole. Clyde caught a towering fly ball on the foul side of third for the last out of the inning.

The score remained 3-1 for three additional innings as the two hurlers settled down and pitched to spots and kept the hitters off stride. Both teams made some outstanding plays to keep the fans on the edge of their seats. They were playing championship softball—no errors, and quick, sharp action filled with outstanding performances.

Leaping Frog and Rand received loud rounds of applause after great plays in the field. Rand raced nearly to the outfield grass to stop a well hit ball, then from his knees threw the runner out by a half-step. Leaping Frog took an infield hit away from the Buffaloes' clean-up hitter when she swooped down on a high pop-up over the pitching mound and caught the ball inches off the ground.

The score stayed at 3-1 until the last half of the fifth inning. Then, Garden City scored another run when two well-placed fly balls fell between Matt and Patt to cut the deficit to one run.

Clyde and Leaping Frog led a sixth-inning rally. Clyde banged a double through the middle and Leaping Frog slammed an ankle-level inside float-ting lob down the line for a home run. Rand jumped off the bench and threw himself at Clyde crossing the plate. The boys were lying in a heap inches from the plate when Leaping Frog trotted in from third base toward home. She stepped on home plate and pulled Rand from the ground. A silly expression seemed painted on her face. She didn't say a word as she put both arms around him and planted a kiss on his lips.

Rand didn't say a word either—just looked back at his shortstop, and a second group of butterflies joined the softball butterflies circling in his stomach.

Strangely, as he looked at Leaping Frog, he saw something new—the face of a girl, not a shortstop —a dark-haired, dark-eyed girl. And as he watched her, the butterflies reared back up and banged into his rib cage.

"Hey, you guys, quit moonshining over each other," barked Clyde, pulling Rand away. "Remember, we've got a ball game to win. Remember?" He poked Rand, and looked curiously at Leaping Frog. Then he rolled his eyes skyward. "Oh, NO!"

Fortunately for the Ludell Leapers, the Garden City Buffaloes didn't score in the last half of the sixth inning and the tally remained 5-2. They grounded out to Clyde at third and hit two pop-ups to the infield. The Leapers went down in order in the top of the seventh and the state championship came down to the last half inning and nothing had really been settled yet. If anything, things seemed a little more confused for the Ludell Leapers.

Rand had been a pepperbox, but as he trotted to his position at second, his mind was clouded by the image of the shortstop playing beside him. No more did thoughts of Tom Seaver, the New York Mets, or the state championship dance in his head. Instead, he watched a young Indian girl float across his mind. He tried to blink out the new image, but a crack of the bat interrupted. He saw a streaking ball to his left. He hesitated to make sure it was real. Then he moved, dove, but missed the ball by inches. He climbed to his feet, dusted himself off, and cast an agonized look at Clyde and Leaping Frog.

Willie followed up seconds later with his first really bad pitch of the game, a hanging spinning lob to the clean-up hitter, who promptly knocked it out of the ball park to cut the Ludell lead, 5-4.

The next hitter flied out for the first out, but the third baseman drilled one through the infield for a clean hit. Rand found his eyes wandering toward Leaping Frog as the next hitter stepped in.

Willie flipped the next pitch, unaware of Rand's lack of attention, and the hitter slammed a ground ball up the middle. Rand lost a half-step because he didn't see the ball until it was almost through the infield. However, Leaping Frog raced far to her left to knock the ball down. Rand instinctively recovered and raced over to where Leaping Frog was lying on the ground with the ball inches away.

"The ball. The ball!" yelled Clyde. "Pick up the ball!"

Leaping Frog was up and grabbing the ball, but it was too late to throw the runner out at first. The runner raced around to third to put the tying run in scoring position with only one out.

And, as if fate had suddenly taken a hand to determine the outcome, the next hitter was fooled on an inside pitch but did manage to loft a Texas Leaguer down the first base line, inches away from Tommy and Matt. The ball took a crazy hop to evade both players. By the time Matt got the ball back into the infield, the runner at first, looking like a green-and-yellow grasshopper, had streaked around second and third. He ran across home plate with the game-winning run and the state championship.

In a short five minutes, the Ludell Leapers had

"Pick up the ball!"

seen a state championship slip through their fingers. Heartsick, they walked off the field and back to their cars for the long ride home. Shouts from the Garden City players and loud music from the pep band echoed across the Kansas plains. But tonight—there was no joy in the air for the Ludell Leapers.

Chapter 15

It had been six days since the Ludell Leapers lost the state softball championship game. Rand was in his room packing for the trip back to New York. To him, the summer had closed on somewhat of a sour note, but he felt more empty than bitter. He had bid all of his teammates farewell the day before, except for Leaping Frog, and he was surprised at how well everyone had taken the loss. They had accepted it, just as Clyde had said they would. No one mentioned Rand's two mental lapses, which actually had cost the Leapers the championship.

Willie had told him, "It's just a game of inches and we were just a quarter inch or so away from being state champs . . . and that ain't bad in anybody's book."

And, probably for the first time in Rand's life, he realized that softball, or baseball, or whatever game it was, was only a contest—not a life-and-death struggle.

Still, the memory of those butterflies, the ones that had first entered his life after Leaping Frog kissed him, was more vivid than anything else. He wanted desperately to see her before he left, but he really didn't know what to say to a shortstop who had turned from a buddy to a kissable member of the opposite sex.

Rand stuffed a few last items in his duffel and looked at his watch. The plane was leaving in several hours and they still had to drive sixty miles to the nearest airport. He wondered where Clyde was and started toward the door of his room. He stopped suddenly and blinked his eyes to get a clearer picture of the figure standing there. He blinked again and the image came into focus.

Rand looked down at the floor and slowly raised his eyes to make sure his vision was not playing tricks on him. His glance took in a pair of black boots, a white mini-skirt, a halter top. He looked slowly on up into dark eyes and became speechless. He still couldn't adjust to the change. The butterflies raced from the pit of his stomach to his throat.

Leaping Frog grinned at Rand and stepped aside to let Clyde come into the room. "Thought our shortstop ought to say good-bye," said Clyde. He put his hands in his back pockets. "It wouldn't have been much of a summer without you and Leaping Frog." He started to slap her on the back, but stopped his hand in mid-flight.

The three stared awkwardly at each other for several minutes, and then Clyde excused himself, muttering something about seeing if his parents were almost ready for the drive to the airport.

Leaping Frog walked closer to Rand. "I've only got a few minutes before the bus comes through Ludell. I'm going home to the reservation to get ready for school." She moved still closer. "I just wanted to see you and tell you some things before I left." Her voice broke, and she poked at the corner of her eye. "I've never had so much fun in a summer in my life. You've been . . . well . . . you've just been something special!"

Quickly she encircled Rand in a giant hug. "Kickapoos never say good-bye. We just say *Pa-Ma-Meen-A*. Till I See You Again!"

Then Leaping Frog smiled shyly and repeated, more to herself than to Rand, *"Pa-Ma-Meen-A."*

She bolted from the room suddenly, and out of the house. Rand ran to the bedroom window and saw her hop into the black pickup, where Tom

126

Frog was waiting to take her to the bus stop in town. She leaned out and waved.

"Pa-Ma-Meen-A," Rand shouted out the window. "Till I See You Again!"

Rand watched the old pickup rattle out of the yard, down the road, past the stubble of wheat fields and past tumbleweeds piled against barbed-wire fences. A frog joined the butterflies in his throat. Slowly he picked up his duffel and walked out the bedroom door, closing it behind him.

The wind, stirred by the door's movement, lifted a yellowed magazine cover of Tom Seaver, stuck in a far corner of a dresser mirror, and pulled it gently to the floor.

ABOUT THE AUTHOR

RONALD G. BLISS was born in Atwood, Kansas, and has followed sports closely from his sandlot days in Northwest Kansas. He holds a journalism degree from Kansas State University and an M.A. from the University of Missouri. He has worked as a reporter for the Findlay, Ohio, *Republican-Courier,* as news editor of the Colby, Kansas, *Free Press-Tribune,* and as a radio-TV specialist for the University of Missouri. He is currently an investigative reporter for KSN, a television network, and one of his documentaries, a look at child abuse, was cited by the Kansas Association of Broadcasters as the best television documentary of 1972. He has published in *TV Guide, V.F.W. Magazine,* and many other magazines. He lives in Maize, Kansas, with his wife, Janie, and two sons, Eric and Kirk.

ABOUT THE ARTIST

WILLIAM MOYERS has been a cowboy, a rodeo rider, a schoolteacher, and an animator for Walt Disney. He now devotes most of his time to painting, specializing in canvases of the West, and to sculpture. Mr. Moyers is married, and he and his wife and four children live in Albuquerque, New Mexico.

DATE DUE

JAN 15 1979			
GAYLORD			PRINTED IN U.S.A